OZ USA
THERE'S A ZOMBIE IN MY CLOSET
I0719277

THE BLACK DIAMOND EFFECT® ....Volume 1, No. 35
THERE'S A ZOMBIE IN MY CLOSET! (Digest Edition)

THE BLACK DIAMOND EFFECT® is a federal registered trademark of George Peter Gatsis.
All prominent characters featured in the book and the distinctive likeness thereof are
trademarks of George Peter Gatsis unless otherwise noted.

"TBDE" is an abbreviation of THE BLACK DIAMOND EFFECT®.

Critical Blast Publishing
24 Hillside Drive Suite A,
Holiday Island, AR 72631

Created, Story, Book Design, Typesetting, Cover Art & Interior Illustrations by George Peter Gatsis.
© 2024 George Peter Gatsis. All Rights Reserved. GeorgePeterGatsis•com

Written by R.J. Carter. All Rights Reserved.

First Edition July 2024

0 9 8 7 6 5 4 3 2 1

ISBN: 978-1-895462-93-7   (Digest Edition)

Distributed by Critical Blast Logistics - CriticalBlast.com / PRINTED IN USA.

CLOSET
THERE'S A ZOMBIE IN MY
OZ USA

THERE'S A
ZOMBIE IN
MY CLOSET!

introduction

In the shadowy corners of our homes, a mysterious space serves as a stage for chaos. From the daily struggle of finding matching shoes to the surprise appearances of forgotten items, this realm never fails to amaze, entertain and scare! That place is known as: the closet.

Cynthia's Bedroom

Enter a small, cozy bedroom with pastel-colored walls and stuffed animals strewn across the floor. A soft pink bedspread lays crumpled where Cynthia had been sleeping. She stirred, yawning and rubbing her eyes, her messy jet black hair framing her face.

As she got out of bed, a strange, muffled noise caught her attention. It was coming from the closet.

Curious and a bit apprehensive, she flicked the light switch.

The light didn't work. She grabbed a flashlight and tiptoed towards the closet door. The noise grew louder, and with a hesitant hand, she turned the handle and pulled it open.

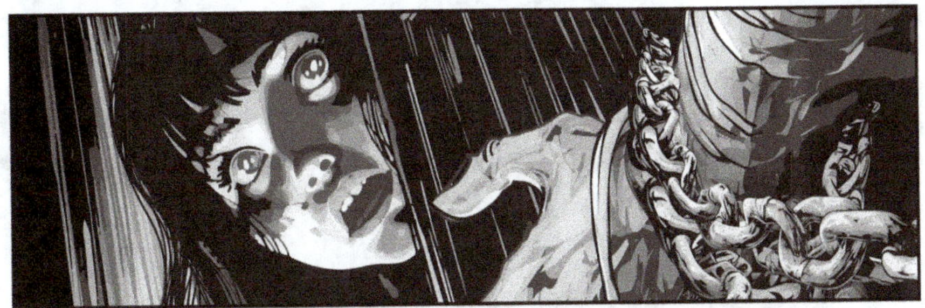

To her horror, a ZOMBIE, pale and grotesque, lunged towards her, its arms outstretched. Cynthia screamed, tripped over her own feet, and kicked the door shut in a panic. Breathing heavily, she took a quick peek inside again, only to find the zombie still there.

She slammed the door shut and bolted from her room.

The Living Room

Downstairs, her dad, a man in his early forties, was engrossed in a video game. The living room was cluttered with books, toys, and remnants of yesterday's meals, all centered around an unusually sophisticated TV screen.

"Dad!" Cynthia called out, skidding to a halt next to the couch. "Dad, where's Mom?"

Without looking away from the screen, her dad replied, "She went out to get pizza. Wanted to save on the delivery charge."

"For breakfast?" the girl asked incredulously.

"Honey, you slept in. It's the afternoon," he said, still not glancing her way.

"Dad, there is a zombie in my closet," she blurted out, her voice trembling.

"Yes, honey bunny," he murmured, absorbed in his game.

The girl waited, hoping for a more serious response, but none came. Frustrated, she sat beside him. "Why is there a zombie in the closet?"

Her dad continued playing, his eyes fixed on the screen. "Because I ran out of room in the garage."

Her mouth dropped open. "What's in the garage?"

"More zombies," he said nonchalantly.

"Dad, why are you collecting zombies?" she asked, her confusion growing.

"So I can use them against the aliens," he replied matter-of-factly.

"Of course," she muttered, rolling her eyes. "Wait, what aliens?"

Her dad pointed to the living room window. "The ones trying to take over the world."

The girl rushed to the window and pulled back the curtains. Her eyes widened in shock at the chaotic scene outside:

alien spaceships fired lasers, people ran screaming, explosions rocked buildings, and giant robots battled the invaders.

"Holy smokes! I'm dreaming. I must be dreaming."

"Nope. You're awake," her dad's voice came from behind her.

She ran back to him, shaking his arm urgently. "Dad, this is not the time to play games! And when did you get a game system? I thought we couldn't afford it."

"You're making me miss my shots," he complained, trying to focus on the game. "Pumpkin, relax. I got this," he said, leaning forward for better aim. "While you were asleep, the aliens invaded earth. Their weapons don't kill humans; they turn them into zombies. And it turns out, the aliens are allergic to zombies."

"Why didn't you wake me?" she demanded.

"You went to sleep late and you looked so cute sleeping. I didn't have the heart to wake you," he explained. "Oh, and since humanity has been preparing for the zombie apocalypse since 'Night of the Living Dead,' we used the zombies against them."

"So that is why you have stashed zombies in our house?" she asked.

"Yep. Made a lot of noise, but you didn't wake up. You're so cute when you sleep," he said, his tone affectionate.

"Yeah, I know, asleep," she replied, rolling her eyes again. "So, what? You're waiting for the aliens to come to us and then you'll unleash the zombies like guard dogs?"

"Exactly," he said, smiling at her.

"But why play a video game? Why not go out there and fight the aliens?" she asked, confused.

"Honey bunny, that's what I am doing! During the night, one of the aliens controlling a giant robot was attacked by zombies, and I brought its control system home," he explained. "By the way, the aliens don't have any bone structure. The zombies just bit into them, and they squirted ooze, like jelly-filled balloons."

"Dad, focus!" she shouted, exasperated.

"Like shooting fish in a barrel," he said, as if explaining a simple task.

"Wowzers!" she exclaimed, impressed despite herself.

He handed her the controller. "Here, take over for me."

She took the controller, tentatively pressing the buttons. "It's simple. The stick is for movement. The buttons shoot missiles, lasers, and bombs."

He kissed her on the forehead and stood up. "What are you going to do?" she asked.

"Bathroom break before your mom gets home," he replied.

"Wait, Dad!" she shouted, as he reached the entrance to the living room. "Mom is out there, in all that craziness! She'll get killed!"

"Duh. That's what the robot's for. I was laying down covering fire for her on the way to get the pizza," he said.

She looked closer at the screen and saw a woman on a motorcycle, dodging alien fire while carrying a pizza box. "Mom?"

"Lay down covering fire as your mom's coming home. Make sure you aim before firing," he instructed, leaving the room.

Taking a deep breath, she focused on the screen, determined to protect her mother. As she got into the groove of controlling the giant robot and fighting off aliens, a sense of responsibility and courage washed over her. She wasn't just playing a game; she was part of the fight, protecting her family in the middle of an alien invasion.

ADVERTISING

Introduction

In the bustling world of transportation, the enigmatic metal box reigns supreme. This unassuming contraption, often filled with strangers trying desperately to avoid eye contact, serves as a stage for a myriad of cringe-worthy performances. From the accidental button-pushing frenzy to the uncomfortable private whispered conversations, the metal box never fails to entertain and bewilder its captive audience.

The Elevator

The elevator arrived with a soft "bing," and its doors slid open to reveal an empty cabin. A man stepped inside, glancing around curiously. His eyes were drawn to the large advertising monitor on the back wall. As he reached to press the floor buttons, he noticed there were only five options: EMERGENCY, DOORS OPEN, DOORS CLOSED, UP, and DOWN. He chuckled, looking back at the bustling lobby.

With a shrug, he pressed the UP button. The doors slammed shut, and the elevator began its rapid ascent.

At floor 365, the advertising monitor flickered to life, displaying a commercial about newborn babies. The man steadied himself against a side wall as the elevator's speed increased. Panic set in, and he repeatedly pressed the emergency button.

"Help! The elevator is out of control! I have a job interview, and I don't want to be late!" he shouted.

A calm voice responded, "Hello, yes?"

"Help! I want to get off now!" the man insisted.

"Sir, our records indicate you are on an express elevator to the top floor," the voice explained.

"I want to speak to your supervisor!" the man demanded.

"I'm sorry, sir. No one is available right now," the voice replied.

A panel slid open on the wall, and a bench folded out. "Please have a seat and enjoy the ride. We have some wonderful videos on the screen that you might like," the voice suggested.

Frustrated, the man punched the wall panel. "This is bogus! I gave up my dream date to get to this interview! You can't do this to me!" Resigned, he sat on the bench as the elevator continued its ascent.

"Calm," he says to himself. "Don't get hot."

At floor 1095, a commercial about baby food played. "Just how high is the top floor?" the man wondered aloud.

Floor after floor, the commercials changed, reflecting different stages of life. At floor 6205, a commercial about dating and STDs appeared. "Oh God, Alice," he muttered, recognizing his own life story unfolding on the screen.

By floor 18,250, the man was on his knees, clutching the screen as a commercial about cancer played, showing a woman in a hospital bed. "This is wrong," he sobbed.

The elevator continued its relentless climb. At floor 29,200, the voice explained, "You came to interview for service in the core. We do background checks on all applicants before the interview."

As the elevator slowed, the man floated briefly above the floor. "These videos were prepared for your ride to the top," the voice added.

At floor 36,500, a commercial about funeral arrangements played as the doors opened to complete darkness. "I seem to have reached the top floor, and it's a black hole. Is that normal?" the man asked.

"I'm sorry, sir. I can only give assistance within the elevator. Floor assistance is a different department," the voice responded.

Frustrated, the man demanded, "I want to go back down to the lobby."

"Yes, sir. Just press the down button," the voice instructed.

He pressed the button, and the elevator descended rapidly, coming to a stop at floor zero. "Bing." The doors opened, revealing the lobby once again.

The man stepped halfway out, then paused and pressed the

emergency button. "You previously said, 'if I want to get to the top floor.' What if I want to get off at another floor?" he asked.

"That is highly unusual, sir," the voice replied.

"Unusual, but not impossible, right?" he insisted.

After a moment of silence, the voice admitted, "We can't let you off at any floors other than the top floor. Allowing you to go back in time is against company policy."

The man thought carefully. "But I'm not asking to go backward in time. I'm asking to go sideways."

There was another pause. "Could you elaborate, sir?"

"You've shown me videos of my entire life. But I haven't lived my entire life yet. I'm 25 years old today," he explained. "Today, I chose to go to a job interview instead of my first date with my childhood crush, Alice. You messed up, and I demand you fix this now. Alice is waiting for me at the metro library."

A moment later, a well-dressed woman entered the elevator. The man moved to the back as she inserted a key into the emergency button, revealing a keypad.

"Are you sure you want floor 9125?" she asked.

The man nodded. "Yes. Yes, please."

She pressed the numbers, and the elevator doors closed. As they ascended, the man sat down, and the woman stood opposite him.

"This doesn't happen often, does it?" he asked.

"It is very rare," she replied.

"I'm going to change. I'm not going to be that man. I'm going to love my wife. You'll see," he vowed.

"Yes, sir. We will see," she said as the elevator stopped at floor 9125. The doors opened to the metro library, where Alice was reading a book.

The woman gestured for him to step out. "Your floor, sir."

"Thank you," he said, stepping off. Alice looked up, smiling, and hugged him. As the elevator doors closed, the woman turned to the screen, which now displayed happier advertisements full of life as the elevator ascended once more.

At floor 34,675, the elevator stopped at a hospital floor. An old man stepped in. "I remember you," he said to the woman.

"Yes, sir," she replied.

"You're here to take me to the top floor, aren't you?" he asked.

"Yes, sir," she confirmed, offering her hands.

"Will they miss me?" he asked, looking back.

"Yes, sir. Very much. And they will remember you," she assured him.

He entered the elevator, and the doors closed. "Will the ride be long?" he asked.

"Bing." Floor 36,500. The doors opened to reveal deep space and a beautiful whirlpool galaxy.

"Well, that was quick," the old man remarked, gazing out. "Well, this is the end, eh?"

The woman smiled. "Oh no, sir. This is not the end. It's only the beginning for you." A huge spaceship appeared, parking close to the elevator. She touched the old man, now transformed into a young man in a spacesuit.

"I don't understand," he said.

"First time around, you didn't qualify. Now you're officer material. Welcome to the service," she said as he stepped toward his new future.

36500

GHOST U

introduction

It was a great day. High school life was nearly over, grades were just good enough to pass, the job interview had gone well, the school basketball team finally had their first victory, and a girl had shown interest. It was a great day! Until that one stroll in the night...

Ghost U

Dave, a senior in high school, strolled down the street at 10:30 pm, whistling and gazing at the stars. A year ago to this minute had marked the last of his happy days.

He giggled and extended his arm out, but his internal monologue turned somber. "I don't even remember what it feels like to laugh."

Suddenly, a scream pierced the night. Dave stopped and turned toward the sound. A woman, frantic and disheveled, struggled down a porch and ran down the driveway, her eyes wild with terror.

"Help! Help me!" she cried, running up to Dave and grabbing at his clothes. "Call 911! Call the police! Call someone!" She patted him down, searching for a phone. "Where's your phone?!"

Dave opened his mouth to speak, but before he could respond, the woman was struck down right in front of him. He watched in slow motion as she hit the pavement, her body twitching before becoming still.

"I don't know what it was that changed me at that moment," Dave reflected. "The shock of seeing someone die right in front of me."

He saw a foot kick the woman's lifeless body and raised his gaze to the house. Standing beside him was a ghost, translucent and menacing. Dave didn't react.

"Or the fact the killer is a ghost, which was standing right beside me," he thought.

The ghost seemed puzzled by Dave's lack of reaction. It waved a hand in front of his face and brought its claws right up to his eyes, searching for any sign of fear. But Dave remained impassive, his gaze drifting between the house and the woman's body.

"Help!" A voice called out from the house. Dave saw Mr. Sawyer crawl out of the front door, bloodied and desperate.

The ghost, now convinced Dave couldn't see it, darted to Mr. Sawyer and killed him with a swift stab to the back. Lights flickered on in the neighborhood houses as neighbors began to stir.

"I kept my mouth shut when they were questioning me," Dave recalled as neighbors rushed out, some calling the police. "I told them I didn't see who killed the Sawyers."

Hours later, Dave sat in an interrogation room at the police station, two officers bombarding him with questions. "Who would believe me? And even if I said something, how would they be able to stop the ghosts from killing me on the spot?" Another ghost hovered beside him, unseen by anyone else.

At 6:30 am, Dave walked out of the police station, his parents thrilled to hug their son. His mother wrapped her arms around him while his Dad patted his back. They walked towards their parked minivan, surrounded by hundreds of ghosts, all watching, waiting for someone to notice them.

"Hundreds!" Dave thought, looking at the spectral figures. "Thousands! All over the world!"

Inside the minivan, Dave's younger sister, Lisa, woke up and smiled when she saw her brother. A ghost hovered next to her, observing for any reaction. When Lisa remained oblivious, the ghost flew away.

"Watching us. And if we see them, kill us," Dave mused. "How do you combat millions of intangible killers? You start by going back to school."

Dave stood in front of the Sawyers' abandoned house, determination replacing his fear. "Ask a question."

In the library, he sifted through documents, hiding them under books about Tesla when a ghost hovered nearby. "Do background research."

At a news station, Dave typed away on a keyboard, writing about unusual deaths. "Construct a hypothesis."

He watched as a ghost hovered near a water cooler, waiting for a woman to finish her drink. When she splashed a sleazy man with water, the ghost dodged the liquid, and the man's phone short-circuited. Dave smiled.

Standing in the rain, Dave held a large umbrella, a ghost hovering under it. "Test your hypothesis by doing an experiment." He let go of the umbrella just as lightning struck, soaking the ghost, which fled for cover. Dave skipped after his umbrella, victorious.

In the basement of the news station, a wall of detailed notes and a checklist of traps, many involving electricity, covered the walls. "Analyze your data and draw a conclusion." Dave nodded to himself, making notes in a blueprint book.

Finally, Dave entered the Sawyer house, dressed in an electrified suit. The first ghost turned to him, and he saluted it, challenging it to a fight. "And communicate your results."

The ghost flew at Dave, who adjusted a frequency dial on his suit and swung an electrified bat. The ghost exploded in a myriad of color smoke, its scream echoing as it vanished.

"Yep, one year ago was the last happy day for me," Dave thought, jotting down his experience in a notebook. "Yep, I love going back to school, so much so, I'm gonna spread that love all around. Yep."

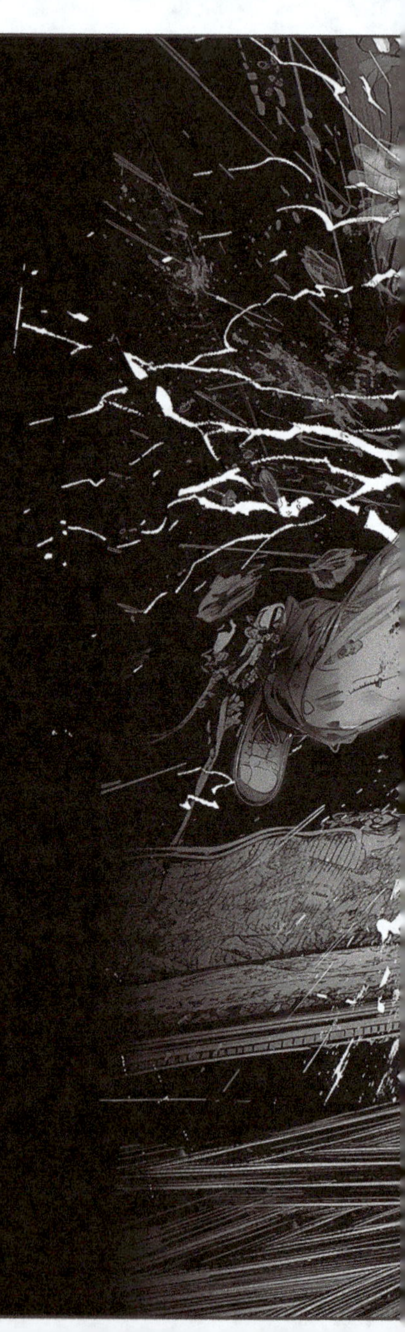

PAPA

Introduction
There are an infinite number of decision point intersections that happen every day in our lives. You could find yourself delayed on public transit and end up bumping into someone you haven't seen in a long time, or just miss buying a winning lottery ticket. One such intersection had already occurred, setting the stage for a chilling discovery...

The Warehouse

In a dimly lit warehouse, the sound of an old clock ticking echoed through the cold, cavernous spacve. An unconscious woman, bound tightly to a wooden chair, began to stir. Nearby, a man methodically unrolled a set of doctor tools on a weathered table, each metal instrument gleaming under the flickering fluorescent lights.

The woman groaned as she regained consciousness. Confusion clouded her eyes as she took in her surroundings. "What's going on? Where am I?" she asked, her voice shaky.

The man glanced at her briefly before returning to his task, laying out his tools with meticulous care. "I was at a bar... drinking," she recalled, struggling against her restraints. Panic surged through her as the memories returned. "You put something in my drink!"

With an unsettling cheerfulness, the man turned and skipped up to her. "Hey, you did ask for a strong drink, didn't you?"

She glared at him. "So what? What are you going to do to me?"

"Guess," he replied with a twisted smile.

"You seem like the kinda guy who's gonna rape me. Right after you beat me up?" she said, her voice dripping with disdain.

The man spun around, almost gleefully. "Wrong you are! Almost," he added with a sinister edge, stepping behind her and placing his hands on her shoulders. "I'm gonna experiment on you before I set you on fire."

A chill ran down her spine as he giggled and circled her. "Oh?" she managed to utter.

"I'm gonna test to see what kind of reaction you have after I give you a very special cough syrup," he explained.

"Well, that doesn't sound so bad. And you couldn't do this in a doctor's office?" she asked, trying to maintain a semblance of calm.

"Yeah, that wouldn't be possible. The animal testing would take at least five years, and then human trials would take another five years. My clients want to be on the store shelves by the end of the year, you know, to maximize their investor returns."

"Yummy. So what are the side effects so far?" she inquired, her voice trembling.

"Oh, the usual. Coughing, dry throat, loss of hunger, vomit, blurry vision, stiffness of joints, shortness of breath, nose bleeds, death or worse," he listed nonchalantly.

"Worse than death?" she echoed, horrified.

"Yeah, you could hallucinate that everyone is trying to kill you and might hurt yourself," he said, his tone almost casual.

"All this for a cough syrup?"

"You should see what they do for eye shadow and lipstick."

"You did this before?" she asked, a sinking feeling in her stomach.

"Right again!"

"You're the guy everyone's looking for? The one who burns the women along with the ID of the next victim," she said, realization dawning on her.

"Right you are again," he confirmed, leaning close to her face.

"Why are you taking such elaborate staging in the death of your victims?" she questioned, curious despite her fear.

"Because I want the police to think they are chasing someone crazy and not me," he said, stepping back and looking around suspiciously.

"What's going on?" he demanded.

"What do you mean?" she asked, feigning innocence.

"Why aren't you crying or begging for your life?" he yelled, frustration evident in his voice.

"Oh please, don't kill me. I'll do anything. Please. Boo hoo," she mocked, her tone dripping with sarcasm.

"This is not right. This is not supposed to happen like this," he muttered, looking around in confusion.

"Like what? You have me tied up. You're in control here," she pointed out.

"You are too calm. You should be screaming and begging for your life!" he shouted, stepping up to her and placing a knife at her throat. "I took off all your clothes and made sure you didn't have anything that could lead the cops here."

"And you redressed me before I awoke? You're such a nice boy," she retorted.

"They are coming, aren't they?" he asked, paranoia creeping into his voice.

"Nope. The cops, the FBI, and everyone else you may think of, is not coming," she stated calmly.

"Then why are you so confident? Why aren't you begging for your life?" he demanded.

"Because, by now the police will have found your last victim's burnt body and my ID," she explained.

"Yeah, so?"

"So, the police will have notified my family."

"Yeah, that's the point. To cause as much pain as I can before I kill you!"

"Yeah, well my Dad won't be thrilled about me being in danger and all."

"Oh, what can your 'Dad,' do? Go on TV and cry and beg for your safe return. Oh, I'm so scared," he mocked.

"Nope. My Dad, has very special friends and when they get here, they will have a very special plan for you."

"Yeah, what kind of plan?"

A humming sound filled the air. The man looked up just as a column of light punched a hole through the ceiling, enveloping him in its brilliance. Frozen within the column, he looked back at the woman in terror.

She saw a tall, slender figure emerge from the light, an alien being with an otherworldly presence. The alien freed her from the chair and placed a gentle kiss on her forehead. She looked back at the man, now paralyzed in the column of light, and calmly walked out of the warehouse.

The alien's face transformed, taking on a fierce and menacing expression. "No one messes with my daughter," it growled, reaching for the man. His screams echoed in the darkness as everything went black.

THE MAN

Introduction

Agent Man, a suave operative, takes on unusual jobs with style. He's the go-to man for unconventional challenges, from infiltrating secret societies to rescuing rich women from boredom. Just don't mention clowns — he has a strict policy against them.

On the Road

The car sped down the highway, rap music blaring from the speakers, as the man behind the wheel received a call. Another job. He jotted down the address and drove off, the credits of his life playing out against the urban backdrop.

As he arrived at the house, he noted the surroundings—an affluent white neighborhood. He tapped his watch, cycling through a series of options: Lamp Post, Garbage Can, Mail Box, Fat White Man, Barrel. He selected Fat White Man, and a hologram enveloped him, projecting the image of a white man. He exited the car and approached the front door, ringing the bell.

An old blind woman answered, her eyes clouded and vacant. "Yes? Hello? You are? Come in," she said, inviting him inside.

The man tapped his watch again, reverting to his original appearance. "You called about a ghost?" he asked.

The old woman seemed confused. "I don't remember ever calling anyone about a ghost. Are you sure you have the right address?" She scratched her head, stepping deeper into the house.

"Maybe I did. Maybe I did. Come in, young man, come in."

He entered cautiously, taking in the decor and the many pictures on the wall. The house exuded history and a sense of time standing still.

"Come in, come in," the woman urged again, leading him to the living room. She settled on the main sofa, a tray of tea and crackers in front of her. "Well, here we are. I don't get many visitors these days. Care for a biscuit?"

"No, thank you," he replied, glancing around. "There is a lot of history here."

A little girl, pale and gaunt like a specter, emerged from the kitchen, ready to take an order. "Would you like anything else we may have to drink or eat?" the old woman asked.

"No, thank you," he said again. The girl vanished back into the kitchen.

"Only two people living here?" he inquired.

"Silly boy, there is no one living in this house," she replied with a chuckle.

The man looked puzzled, stepping near a large mirror that cast no reflection of him. "Come again?"

The old woman picked up a knife beside the teapot and lunged at him, but the blade passed through his body harmlessly. Frustration contorted her face as she looked around in bewilderment.

Ignoring her, the man escorted the little girl out the front door. The old woman screamed and chased after them.

At the front entrance, the woman halted at the door frame, still yelling threats. The man led the girl to his car and placed her in the front passenger seat. She looked up at him, eyes wide with fear. "Are you going to leave me?"

"Nope," he reassured her.

He got into the driver's seat, turned the car, and backed it up with the trunk facing the house. Exiting the car, he stepped to the trunk, which opened to reveal a massive transformer-like speaker system. He cranked the volume to "11" and turned it on.

The blast of music and sound caused the old woman to screech in agony before she disappeared. The force of the sound flipped over a loose sign that read, "This property is abandoned and scheduled for demolition."

The speakers retracted into the car, and the man got back in. The little girl leaned over, gave him a kiss, and disappeared, giggling. Without missing a beat, he put on his sunglasses and drove off, music blaring once more as movie credits of his life roll out in his head.

MORE GREAT BOOKS AVAILABLE AT CRITICAL BLAST PUBLISHING...
GO TO: CRITICALBLAST•COM NOW!
CRITICAL BLAST PUBLISHING
THE BROTHERS GRIMM The Complete Illustrated Fairy Tales
THE WRENCH IN THE MACHINE
THE DEVIL YOU KNOW Edited by R.J. Carter
THE DEVIL YOU KNOW BETTER Edited by R.J. Carter
THE DEVIL YOU KNOW BEST Edited by R.J. Carter
THE BROTHERS GRIMM The Complete Illustrated Fairy Tales
THE MAFIA IN HOLLYWOOD STORIES FROM PRE CODE FILM TO
THE LIFE AND TIMES OF FRANK BALISTRIERI THE LAST, MOST POWERFUL BOSS OF HIS KIND   WAYNE CLINGMAN   ZACK LON
THE BUFFALO MOB
THE BUFFALO MOB THE RETURN OF ORGANIZED CRIME TO THE QUEEN CITY
GODS & SERVICES Carter
gavelockstudio.com
GH057 STORY
gavelockstudio.com
GH057 STORY
gavelockstudio.com
GH057 STORY
THE BLACK DIAMOND EFFECT   JOE KING   JOE ADE   GEORGE PETER GATSIS
INCANTESI BOOK 1 & 2 COLLECTED EDITION by Rich Perrotta
THE BLACK DIAMOND EFFECT by GEORGE PETER GATSIS
GENUINE COMICS — PERFECT 10 ARTIST EDITION
CRITICAL BLAST PUBLISHING COLORS NOT INCLUDED! 01
CRITICAL BLAST PUBLISHING COLORS NOT INCLUDED! 02
THE BUFFALO MOB
THE MONSTERS NEXT DOOR Edited by R.J. Carter
The Fables Next Door
BULLETPROOF
BULLETPROOF
BULLETPROOF Edited By R.J. Carter

ARISTOCRATIC XTRATERRESTRIAL TIME-TRAVELING THIEVES COMPLETE COLLECTION
by David Anthony Kraft & Henry Vogel
• 338 pages

Fred and Bianca, the heroes of the cult classic 1980s parody comic, ARISTOCRATIC XTRATERRESTRIAL TIME-TRAVELING THIEVES are back in this collected edition. Experience the magic all over again as our plucky thieves steal the most culturally significant of items.

"This is one of the best of the funny comic books (and one of the handful that really is funny)."
— Don Thompson, Comics Buyer's Guide

AVAILABLE IN HARDCOVER / PAPERBACK / DIGEST

THE DEVIL YOU KNOW
edited by R.J. Carter
• 370 pages

A short-story anthology of encounters with various incarnations of The Devil, with genres ranging from fairy tale to folk tale, from urban fantasy to science fiction, from comedy to horror. Featuring the works of Jared Baker, Erica Ciko Campbell, Sarah Cannavo, Michael W. Clark, Christopher Cook, Andra Dill, Cara fox, R.A. Goli, Gerald A. Jennings, Kevin Kangas, Daryl Marcus, Damascus Mincemeyer, Steve Oden, Evan Purcell, Troy Riser, Joseph Rubas, Hannah Trusty, Wondra Vanian, Henry Vogel, and K.D. Webster.

AVAILABLE IN PAPERBACK

THE DEVIL YOU KNOW BETTER
edited by R.J. Carter
• 382 pages

The next volume chronicling the meet-ups between everyday people and The Devil himself. Collecting fantastic tales from Mike Baron, .Ravenna Blazecroft, Richard J. Brewer, Hart D. Fisher, L.N. Hunter, Charlie Jones, Ken MacGregor, James Maxey, Tim McDaniel, Damascus Mincemeyer, Lena Ng, Diana Olney, P. Anthony Ramanauskas, Troy Riser, Edward R. Rosick, Nadia Steven Rysing, Rose Strickman, Anna Taborska, Stanley B. Webb and Ray Zacek.

AVAILABLE IN PAPERBACK

THE DEVIL YOU KNOW BEST
edited by R.J. Carter
• 510 pages

Collected here in this ultimate volume of Critical Blast's THE DEVIL YOU KNOW series are 25 stories from new and seasoned voices of horror. Dan Allen, Paul Barile, Patricia Childs, John Di Donna, Sarina Dorie, Tom Folske, Gene Gallistel, Jonathan Garner, Larry Hodges, Jean Jentilet, Martin Klubeck, Kevin Lauderdale, Robert Allen Lupton, Damascus Mincemeyer, Mike Murphy, Diana Olney, Leanbh Pearson, Janice Rider, Troy Riser, AE Steuve, Kristal Stittle, Donald R. Vogel, Sheri White, Ray Zacek.

AVAILABLE IN PAPERBACK

THE MONSTERS NEXT DOOR
edited by R.J. Carter
• 404 pages

Collected here are twenty incredible stories about monsters in the last place you'd expect to find them - - living in your day-to-day life. With a unique presentation style, this book will delight horror fans everywhere!

AVAILABLE IN PAPERBACK

GODS & SERVICES
edited by R.J. Carter
• 205 pages

When old gods need new worshipers, they offer their divinity for sale. Put a little god in your life with this collection of short stories from authors Ross Baxter, Ira Bloom, Laura J. Campbell, Aristo Couvaras, Jon Del Arraz, David J. Pedersen, Zach Smith, Michael Tierney, and Katherine Traylor.

AVAILABLE IN PAPERBACK

THE MAFIA IN HOLLYOOD: STORIES FROM PRE-CODE FILM TO DEEP THROAT
by Wayne Clingman and Douglas Hess
• 162 pages

An introduction into the history of crime in Buffalo
- The beginnings of Mafia activity in the Queen City
- Past and present alleged leaders, soldiers and associates of The Arm and its affiliated operations
- Government sources and witnesses imperative to understanding mob activities
- An introduction to recent criminal activity indicating the Mafia in Buffalo is anything but dormant..

AVAILABLE IN POCKETBOOK

THE RE-IMAGINED ADVENTURES OF A.B. FROST'S BULL CALF

by R.J. Carter & George Peter Gatsis • 80 pages

This blending, rearranged into the sequential art style of a comic book, delivers a side-splitting tale of mischief and mayhem in this epic journey across time and place.

Watch as an encounter with a Bull Calf sparks off a series of events that boggle the mind as a whole new generation of readers gets to discover the wonderful cartoon art of A.B. Frost.

AVAILABLE IN HARDCOVER / PAPERBACK / POCKET BOOK

THE BUFFALO MOB: THE RETURN OF ORGANIZED CRIME TO THE QUEEN CITY

by Wayne Clingman • 92 pages

Experience the seedy relationship between the Mafia and Hollywood, beginning with the Pre-code era up through the filming of Deep Throat and beyond. Clingman and Hess unearth stories about notorious personages like Abner Zwillman, Gus Greenbaum, and Al Capone, and reveal the effect they had on movie-making, both by reputation and by direct interactions.

AVAILABLE IN PAPERBACK

BROTHERS GRIMM: THE COMPLETE ILLUSTRATED FAIRY TALES

edited by R.J. Carter • 540 pages / • 410 pages

The complete fairy tales of Jacob and Wilhelm Grimm, with over 300 vibrant full-color illustrations and large text to bring each tale to vivid life. These are the stories in their original forms, formatted in an easy-to-read design that will promote faster reading and inspire imagination.

AVAILABLE IN HARDCOVER / PAPERBACK

GRAYSKALE

by Pramit Santrav • 68 pages

GraysKale, the trash-talking masked vigilante with the power to control the forces of karma, brings the villains of Glitter City to justice. But when his identity is exposed, his enemies set a trap. Will GraysKale fall for it, or will he save Glitter City – and his girlfriend – from the evil machinations of criminal casino owner, Johnny Singh?

AVAILABLE IN HARDCOVER / PAPERBACK / POCKETBOOK

MELVIN SPECIAL EDITION #1

by Timothy Lee Olson • 36 pages

Melvin is a mercenary hired to save a princess from a dangerous cult. Written by Timothy Lee Olson with art by Sherwin Caayao Saynes. It's science fiction and fantasy in the action adventure style of the pulps!

AVAILABLE IN HARDCOVER / PAPERBACK / POCKETBOOK

THE INCANTESI

by Rich Perrotta • 100 pages

THE INCANTESI is the story of Cassandra Rossi, a dancer from Milan, who discovers her destiny is not only to be the greatest sorceress of all, but also to be the Keeper of THE WRATH, an aggressive, violent branch of the INCANTESI, a coven of wielders of the mystic arts. THE WRATH fought back against witch hunters, but their bloodlust consumed them and they began killing anyone they could find. The few INCANTESI remaining created an extradimensional prison for THE WRATH, a prison that contained them for 500 years... until now.

AVAILABLE IN HARDCOVER / PAPERBACK / POCKETBOOK

2100 SAMURAI: BIG TROUBLE IN NEO DETROIT

by Nick Gibson • 64 pages

When the young samurai Kiro finds himself transported to this far-flung future, he will have to find his own way - or find a guide that can show him the way. When Tyler, a street rat who finds herself on the wrong side of a deal gone bad, is in need of a hero, will these two find what they need? Or die trying...

AVAILABLE IN HARDCOVER / PAPERBACK / POCKETBOOK

CRITICAL BLAST PUBLISHING COLORING BOOK 01
by R.J. Carter & George Peter Gatsis   • 100 pages

Across the multiverse, through the pan-dimensional rift, comes a collection of covers for comic books that don't exist in this universe. Recovered by Critical Blast Publishing, these black and white pages are presented to you to add the colors, to bring to full reality these images that, to this universe, are naught but a dream.

AVAILABLE IN HARDCOVER / PAPERBACK / POCKET BOOK

GHO57 STORY #1: DOUBLE STARS
by Folkenstal and Hoàng Trong Thiên   • 142 pages

When a robot-like outsider named Ghost stumbles into an isolated solar system, he disrupts Mallory Embers' course, sparking a new adventure for them both. But Ghost isn't just any outsider; he's on a mission to find Carabalt, an important mineral for his kind back home. As he searches, a familiar face, one of the Grim Reapers, is hunting him down.

AVAILABLE IN HARDCOVER / PAPERBACK

THE RE-IMAGINED ADVENTURES OF A.B. FROST'S CARLO
by R.J. Carter & George Peter Gatsis   • 78 pages

A unique combination of brand new story told against Frost's original illustrations. This blending, rearranged into the sequential art style of a comic book, delivers a side-splitting tale of mischief and mayhem starring Frost's lovable bedraggled mutt, Carlo.

Watch as Carlo gets into trouble with chickens, cats, farmers, and would-be thieves as a whole new generation of readers gets to discover the wonderful cartoon art of A.B. Frost.

AVAILABLE IN HARDCOVER / PAPERBACK / POCKET BOOK

GHO57 STORY #2: COLD GRAVITY
by Folkenstal and Hoàng Trong Thiên   • 188 pages

On his way back to his home planet, Tressa, Ghost meets his supervisor, Rose, who has bad news: things have worsened for their fellow Tressians. Rose gives him an important mission that puts Ghost in a tough spot. To help the remaining Tressians, Ghost must make a big sacrifice. Knowing how dangerous this mission is, Mallory tries to stop Ghost because it could cost him his life.

AVAILABLE IN HARDCOVER / PAPERBACK

THE RE-IMAGINED ADVENTURES OF A.B. FROST'S STUFF AND NONSENSE
by R.J. Carter & George Peter Gatsis   • 74 pages

A fresh – and often macabre – twist on the master cartoonist's illustrations that accompanied his many humorous poems.

Reframed and rearranged into a graphic novel format, with all new nonsensical poems, this volume reinterprets Frost's images for a new generation of readers, introducing them to the wonderful cartoon art of A.B. Frost.

AVAILABLE IN HARDCOVER / PAPERBACK / POCKET BOOK

GHO57 STORY #3: BROKEN UNITY
by Folkenstal and Hoàng Trong Thiên   • 186 pages

Join Ghost and Mallory on a thrilling journey to meet the Tressians' creators and ask for their help in the current crisis. Along the way, they meet another Great Hero at a space station, whose lack of concern for others deeply troubles Ghost. Get ready for an emotional ride filled with unexpected revelations and challenges as they face their current mission. Will the creators help Ghost and the Tressians? Can Ghost and the other Great Hero find common ground?

AVAILABLE IN HARDCOVER / PAPERBACK

THE RE-IMAGINED ADVENTURES OF A.B. FROST'S BULL CALF
by R.J. Carter & George Peter Gatsis   • 80 pages

This blending, rearranged into the sequential art style of a comic book, delivers a side-splitting tale of mischief and mayhem in this epic journey across time and place.

Watch as an encounter with a Bull Calf sparks off a series of events that boggle the mind as a whole new generation of readers gets to discover the wonderful cartoon art of A.B. Frost.

AVAILABLE IN HARDCOVER / PAPERBACK / POCKET BOOK

THE SHADOW KINGDOM
by Randy Zimmerman and Russ Leach

• 112 pages

In the time before Atlantis sank and the lands of the world were savage and untamed, one man would claim his destiny. Leaving his Atlantean tribe behind and throwing off the shackles of Lemurian bondage, he sailed the seas as a pirate captain before seizing his place as a king. Considered the first Sword and Sorcery story by Robert E. Howard.

AVAILABLE IN PAPERBACK / POCKETBOOK

NANO 13
by Kris Faction and Ron Moscicki

• 48 pages

3000 years ago, the Zzerus invaded Earth and enslaved mankind. Now a group of nano-powered freedom fighters resolve to take their planet back.

AVAILABLE IN PAPERBACK

THE FABLES NEXT DOOR
edited by R.J. Carter

• 360 pages

Once Upon a Time... fantastic things happened to fantastic characters. Unforgettable things. Unforgettable characters. And then the unforgettable was forgotten. What happened to these characters? Where did they go? What did they do? And what's with that curious moving van parked on your street, the one unloading all the odd packages and strange furniture? Could it be that your new neighbors are a part of old stories? Could they actually be... FABLES?

AVAILABLE IN PAPERBACK

THE WRENCH IN THE MACHINE
by Bonsart Bokel

• 440 pages

In 1875, Inspector Ol'Barrow is still coming to terms with the advent of radio dramas when he is confronted by a series of crimes that defy explanation, committed by an otherworldly assassin.

Spurred on by his sense of duty and a desire to redeem himself, Ol'Barrow uncovers a clandestine organization called The Association of Ishtar, who claim to be mere advisors who aid the authorities with the containment of anomalies.

AVAILABLE IN PAPERBACK

MELVIN SPECIAL EDITION #0
by Timothy Lee Olson

• 36 pages

Melvin is a mercenary hired to save a princess from a dangerous cult. Written by Timothy Lee Olson with art by Sherwin Caayao Saynes. It's science fiction and fantasy in the action adventure style of the pulps!

AVAILABLE IN HARDCOVER / PAPERBACK / POCKETBOOK

CASKET GIRLS
by Bonsart Bokel

• 202 pages

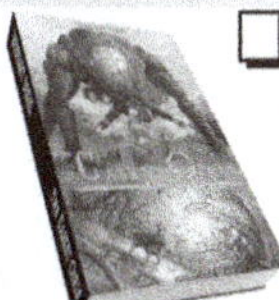

Convicted for their crimes to society, the Casket Girls pilot walking machines called Chassis d'Batteuille to get their sentences reduced. Embark on missions alongside the French Imperial Penal battalions as they confront extraterrestrial invaders emerging from the Rifts appear-ing across the globe.

AVAILABLE IN PAPERBACK

TYGER BLUE
by Matthew Fowler

• 144 pages

Early elements of the Axis Powers are secretly working together to develop the ultimate bio-weapon. Ferocious beasts created by German occult science, trained by dark Samurai, and used by the Mafia as lethal enforcers. When Tyger realizes how truly disposable he is, he rebels against his masters. Forced to fight his brothers, Tyger's struggle for vengeance and survival has begun!

AVAILABLE IN HARDCOVER / PAPERBACK / POCKET BOOK

9 781895 462937